Where the fairies fly

Jane Simmons

ORCHARD BOOKS

To Andrew and Lorna

who like to sleep a lot

ORCHARD BOOKS
96 Leonard Street, London EC2A 4XD
Orchard Books Australia
32/45-51 Huntley Street, Alexandria, NSW 2015
ISBN 1 84121 769 7 (hardback)
ISBN 1 84121 108 7 (paperback)
First published in Great Britain in 2001
First paperback publication in 2001
Copyright © Jane Simmons 2001
The right of Jane Simmons to be identified as the author and
illustrator of this work has been asserted by her in accordance with the
Copyright, Designs and Patents Act, 1988.
A CIP catalogue record for this book is available from the British Library.
(hardback) 10 9 8 7 6 5 4 3 2 1
(paperback) 10 9 8
Printed in Singapore

Lucy loved to
tell stories.

She told deep blue sea stories to Mum . . .

flying up high
in the sky
stories to Dad,

and magic stories to her
little brother Jamie.

But best of all were the stories she told to Bear.
Lucy loved bedtime. She'd hug Bear and whisper
stories until they fell asleep.

But poor Jamie hated bedtime. He'd toss and turn
with Floppy Rabbit and see things in the
shadows on the ceiling.

One night when Jamie was wide awake again,
Lucy said to him, "Bear can't sleep either.
We need to find the Dreamtime Fairies –
they'll help us."

So Lucy, Bear, Jamie and Floppy Rabbit

set off far away across the ocean, to

the land where the fairies fly.

They landed on a rock.
"Turtle!" said Jamie.

"We can't sleep," said Lucy, "so we're looking for the fairies."
"The Dreamtime Fairies?" said Turtle. "They're very shy.
You'll have to look very hard to find them.
Turtles sleep in the sun, why don't you?"
"We could try," Lucy said
and they all lay
in the sun.

Turtle fell asleep, Bear and
Floppy Rabbit fell asleep, but,
"Too hot!" said Jamie.

"Come on," said Lucy, "let's find the fairies."

Jamie heard something move
high up in the trees.
"Tiger!" he said.
"We can't sleep," said Lucy, "so
we're looking for the fairies."

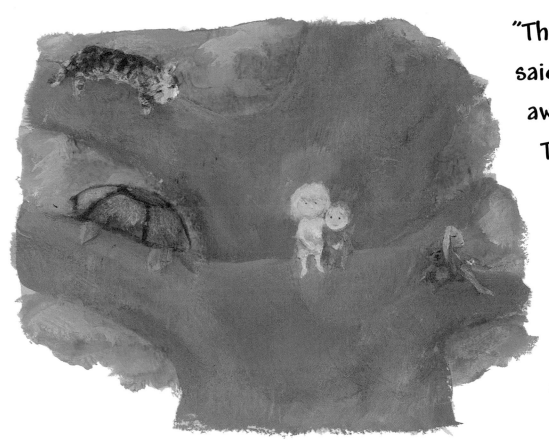

"The Dreamtime Fairies?" said Tiger. "They live far away in the forest. Tigers sleep in trees. Why don't you?"

"We could try," said Lucy and they all climbed up, shut their eyes and rocked in the branches.

Tiger fell asleep, Bear and Floppy Rabbit fell asleep, even Turtle fell asleep, but, "Too high!" said Jamie.

"Come on," said Lucy, "let's find the fairies."

They saw two eyes shining in a deep dark cave.

"Foxy!" shouted Jamie.

"We can't sleep," said Lucy, "so we're looking for the fairies."

"The Dreamtime Fairies?" said Foxy. "They live in the shadows, down in the darkness. Foxes sleep in cosy dark holes, why don't you?"

"It's too dark," said Jamie.

"But we'll have to go into the shadows to find the fairies," said Lucy. "Come on, we'll hold hands!"

So Lucy, Jamie, Bear, Floppy Rabbit, Turtle, Tiger and Foxy followed the path as it twisted and turned. Down they went, down into the forest, down into the darkness, deep down to where the shadows grow.

Jamie stopped. He thought
he heard something in
the shadows . . .
   "Shh!" went Lucy.
They all stood absolutely
still, hardly daring
to breathe . . .

Jamie thought he saw
something, something
moving in the shadows . . .

"Fairies," whispered Jamie.
First there was one shimmer,
then another, and another . . .

until soon the fairies
were all around them,
swooping and dancing
and laughing.

They danced and played
as the fairies **fluttered**
and **twinkled.**

"There's no need to be afraid of the shadows, Jamie," said Lucy. "Because that's where the Dreamtime Fairies fly."

And then they fell on to a pile of leaves covered in soft fairy shadows.

The fairies fluttered and twinkled and worked their Dreamtime magic.

And one by one, first Jamie, then
Floppy Rabbit, then Turtle, Tiger and Foxy,
then Bear and then finally Lucy . . .

gently slipped into the magic of sweet dreams.